Biff made an aeroplane.

1

Mum helped her.

The aeroplane looked good.

Biff wanted to fly it.

She went to the park.

The aeroplane flew up.

6

It went over the trees.

It went over the houses.

9

Biff looked for the aeroplane.

10

Everyone helped.

Biff looked and looked.

She couldn't find it.

She wanted to cry.

14

She went upstairs.

The aeroplane was on the bed.